THE BAD GUYS

EPISODE 9 EPISODE 10

SCHOLASTIC

Published in the UK by Scholastic Children's Books, 2020
Euston House, 24 Eversholt Street, London, NW1 1DB
A division of Scholastic Limited

London – New York – Toronto – Sydney – Auckland
Mexico City – New Delhi – Hong Kong

SCHOLASTIC and associated logos are trademarks and/or
registered trademarks of Scholastic Inc.

Bad Guys Episode 9: The Big Bad Wolf first published in Australia
by Scholastic Australia, 2019
Bad Guys Episode 10: The Baddest Day Ever first published in Australia
by Scholastic Australia, 2019

Text and illustration copyright © Aaron Blabey, 2019

Design by Nicole Stofberg and Sarah Mitchell

The right of Aaron Blabey to be identified as the author and
illustrator of this work has been asserted by him.

ISBN 978 0702 30402 6

A CIP catalogue record for this book is available from the British Library.

Printed by CPI Group (UK) Ltd, Croydon, CR0 4YY
Papers used by Scholastic Children's Books are made
from wood grown in sustainable forests.

3 5 7 9 10 8 6 4 2

www.scholastic.co.uk

AARON BLABEY

THE BAD GUYS

EPISODE 9
THE BIG BAD WOLF

CHAPTER 1

NOW WHAT?

RESTROOM

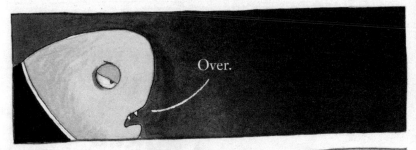

Over.

We can't do this without Wolf.

Without Wolfie, we're . . . nothing.

That ain't true, honey . . .

But it is!

Wolf made **EVERYTHING SEEM POSSIBLE.**

Without him, we're just

A BUNCH OF CROOKS.

And without him leading the way . . .

. . . you feel lost.

I get it. But . . .

No buts!

There's *nothing* you can say to make this better, señorita.

The **ALIENS** have taken over the world,

Wolf is **TOO BIG** and

TOO LOCO to be stopped,

and **ALL HOPE IS LOST!**

Full respect to you and the League of Heroes but *no-one in the world could make this seem OK!*

Someone could.

Wolf could.

You're right, man.
We were nothing without Wolf.
But now . . .

we're *something*
because of Wolf.

And just because he's
**KNOCKING DOWN
SKYSCRAPERS** with his bare hands
and **PARTYING WITH THE ALIENS,**
doesn't give us the right
to give up.

Do you think *he'd* give up?

Or do you think he'd open his **BIG, STUPID MOUTH** and say something idiotic like—

'Hey, Piranha! You've got **SUPER SPEED!** That's a big deal, hermano!'

Or— 'Shark! You're a **SHAPE-SHIFTER,** dude! Disguise yourself as something that will get us out of this mess!'

Or— 'Legs! What do we do here? You're the smartest **NON-VELOCIRAPTOR** I know!'

He really is!

And then he'd say—
'Aren't you all forgetting the

INTERNATIONAL LEAGUE OF HEROES?'

Finally.

'They are the
**BEST OF
THE BEST!**'

Yes, we are.

And so are we!

Ah, no.
No, that's . . .
No.

Aw, let him have this one.

Preach, baby!

So we don't get to give up. We owe it to that numbskull to *never* give up.

We *owe* him.

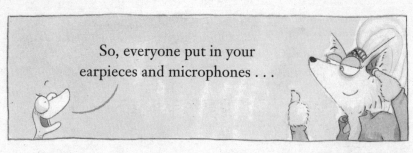

So, everyone put in your earpieces and microphones . . .

This is how it's going down—
HALF OF US
need to keep going with
OPERATION TARANTULA.
We need to get our eight-legged buddy and
Agent Shortfuse onto that **MOTHERSHIP.**
Legs has to **TAKE CONTROL**
of that thing. It's the only way we'll
stop those aliens.

Half of us?!
But what do the
OTHER HALF do?

The other half will
be participating in

**OPERATION
FURBRAIN.**

It's time to get
our big, hairy
buddy back.

· CHAPTER 2 ·
GOODBYE, FOR NOW

That hombre is *big!*
You'll never get any closer than this.
What's your **PLAN,** chico?

That's not your problem.
Your problem is to get
THOSE TWO onto that
MOTHERSHIP.

Good luck, guys.

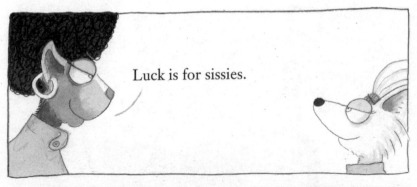

So, what *is* your plan exactly?

Watch this . . .

Wolf.
You will do as I command . . .

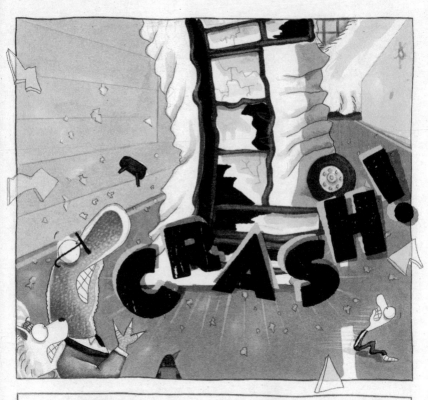

Your plan is to watch him **THROW BUSES?** What? Are you hoping he'll just get sore arms and take a power nap?

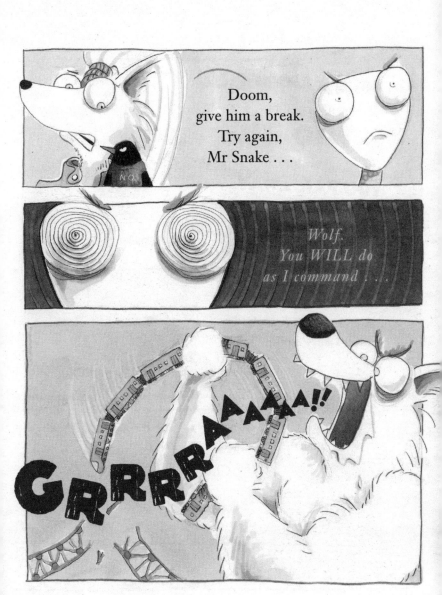

Your name's *Joy?!*

I'll get you for this.

Oh, shoosh.

Mr Snake, I think we need to **DISTRACT** Mr Wolf, to **GET YOU CLOSER...**

Any ideas?

· CHAPTER 3 ·
NEW WINGS

OK, *listen up!*
That alien trash **BLEW UP MY JET**
so we have to get ourselves one of those
ZIPPY LITTLE SPACESHIPS—
THAT'S how we get to the big one.

NO STANDING

so I can fire you both **ONTO THAT MOTHERSHIP.** Then I'll fly the rest of us back here. Any questions?

Well, yes . . . I . . .

Good! Then let's **MOVE OUT!**

There's one!

We'll never get near it. There are too many aliens . . .

Too many?!
You're looking at the
piranha that defeated a
TYRANNOSAURUS REX!

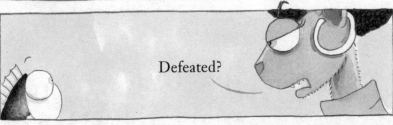

Defeated?

I thought you just got
**STUCK IN ITS
NOSTRIL . . .**

ENOUGH OF THIS TALK!
You must **'BORROW'
THAT SPACESHIP**
and save the world, amigos . . .

Well, what do
you want?
An invitation?

Let's 'borrow' that
spaceship . . .

· CHAPTER 4 ·
IN ONE EAR...

MR WOLF!

MR WOLF?

Mr Wolf?
It's me. It's Agent Fox . . .

That sounds a bit formal, doesn't it? *Agent Fox.* It's funny . . . I just realised . . .

I've never told you my real name, have I?

Well, it's high time I did. Allow me to introduce myself, Mr Wolf. My name is . . .

MR WOLF!
NO!

51

Mr Snake!
This is your chance.
Quick!
NO
This is a *very* bad idea . . .
ROOFTOP STAIRS
GO!
GO!
GO!

So . . .

It was pretty lame
getting to know you.

Thanks.
I feel the same.

Try not to die,
I guess.

Yeah.
You too . . .

Joy.

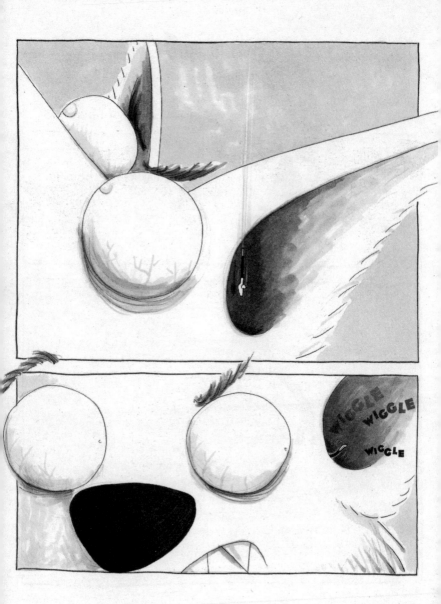

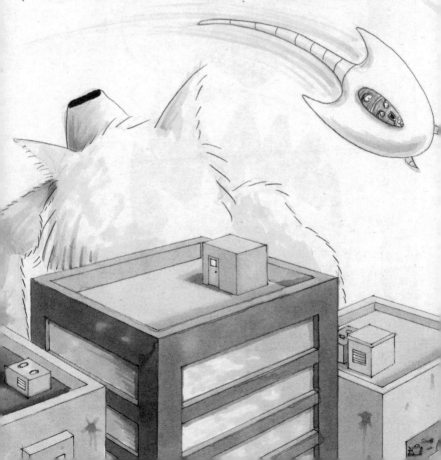

CHAPTER 5

OPERATION TARANTULA

ZOOOOM!

EEEEEEEEEEE!!

They're onto us! We'll never make it!

Not with *you* flying!
Give me that stick,

LITTLE MISS MUFFET.

But . . .
I've only been teaching
you for about 30 seconds . . .

flick!

Well, guess what?
It's **GRADUATION DAY!**
MOVE IT!

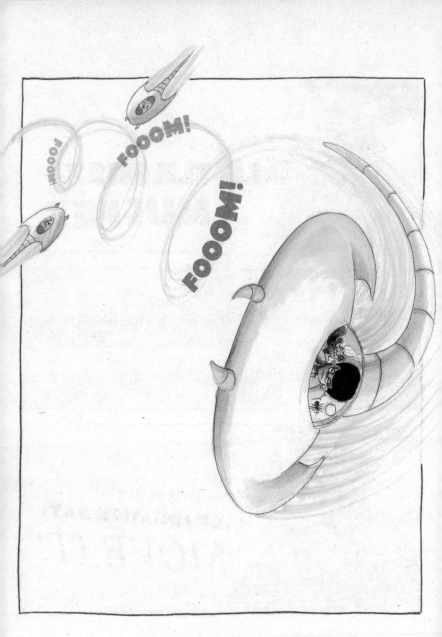

She's a really fast
learner . . .

Now, GET INTO YOUR CONTAINER!
I'm going to launch you onto
the Mothership from the

GARBAGE CHUTE.

But won't they see us launch?
We'll be sitting ducks . . .

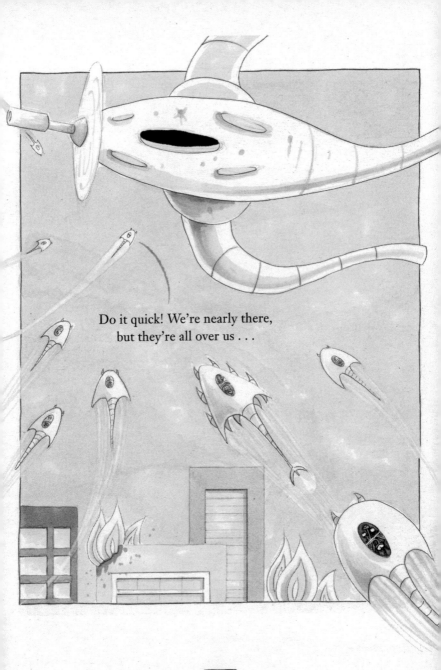

Do it quick! We're nearly there,
but they're all over us . . .

BLOW IT OUT OF THE SKY!

COPY THAT. SHOOTING THE UNICORN ON THREE.

ONE...

Here goes nothing . . .

GULP!

FOOOOP!

PTOOOEEEYY!!!

Bullseye.

TWO...

Hold on,
you big, beautiful,
sparkly pony . . .

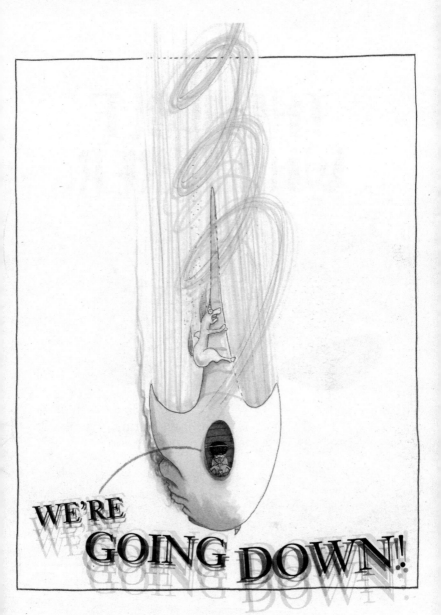

· CHAPTER 6 ·
THE WOLF WHISPERER

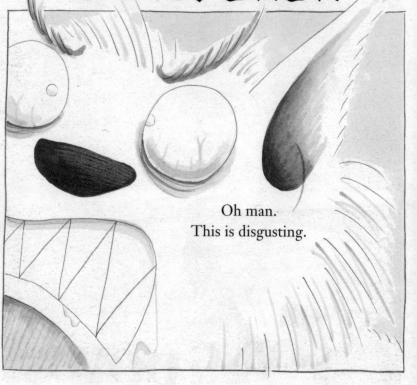

Oh man.
This is disgusting.

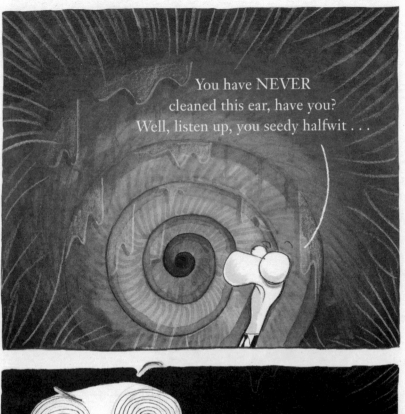

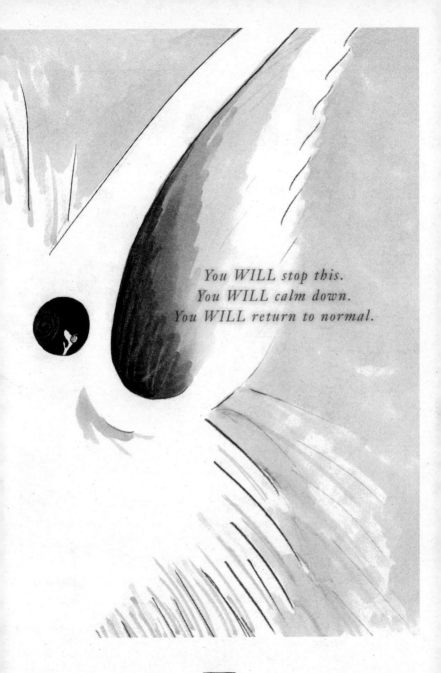

You WILL stop this.
You WILL calm down.
You WILL return to normal.

Mr Snake? Can you hear me?
Just KEEP AT IT!

I can't do it . . .

Just *try*. You have to try.

Soooo sorry to interrupt,
but I fear we may have a teensy,
weensy **PROBLEM** . . .

What is it?!

Well. I just upgraded to some high-quality **HEADPHONES** because those little **EARBUDS** you're all wearing won't be comfortably accommodated by my **PRIMORDIAL EAR HOLES.**

It's been quite a trial.
But fear not, these new ones
are really quite excellent . . .

HOW IS THIS RELEVANT?!

Well, that's the thing. These headphones are of such a high standard, that they seem to have picked up on **ANOTHER SIGNAL** coming from Mr Wolf's enormous head.

What kind of signal . . . ?

Well. Unless I'm *very* much mistaken, I suspect there's **SOMEONE ELSE** lurking about in his **OTHER EAR.**

CHAPTER 7

WHO NEEDS SUPERPOWERS?

Not bad, Agent Hogwild.
We make a pretty good team.

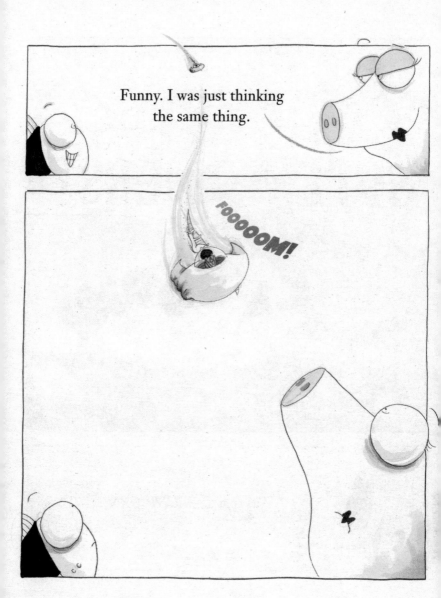

 Was that a . . . *UNICORN?!*

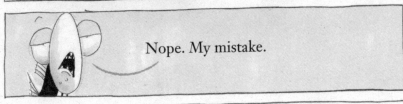

Nope. My mistake.

HELP!

Welcome back, guys, but we'd better move.

FOX IS IN TROUBLE . . .

Thank goodness you're here!
Things have taken a
turn for the worse . . .

WOLF! DESTROY!

Forget you have mind powers for a minute.
Just pretend you're
PLAIN OLD MR SNAKE.

WHAT?
What good will that do?!

That way you can just talk to him.
He loves you.
Just . . . *talk to him.*

But that's . . .

Hey, Wolf?

Yeah I'm talking to *you*, Butt Brain.

Look, man, enough's enough. I'm waist-deep in earwax here

and my patience has **RUN OUT.**

What you're doing is **BAD.** Do you hear me?

You're behaving like a **BAD GUY.**

And at this point, that is *very* disappointing, dude.

So for our sake, and for the sake of

everything you've worked for . . .

I need you to **CUT IT OUT.**

· CHAPTER 8 ·
THE FALL

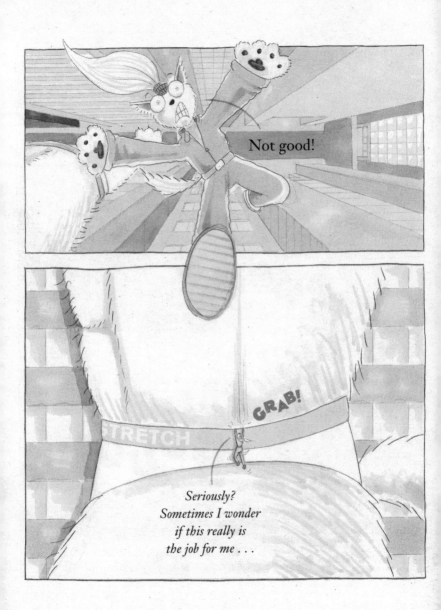

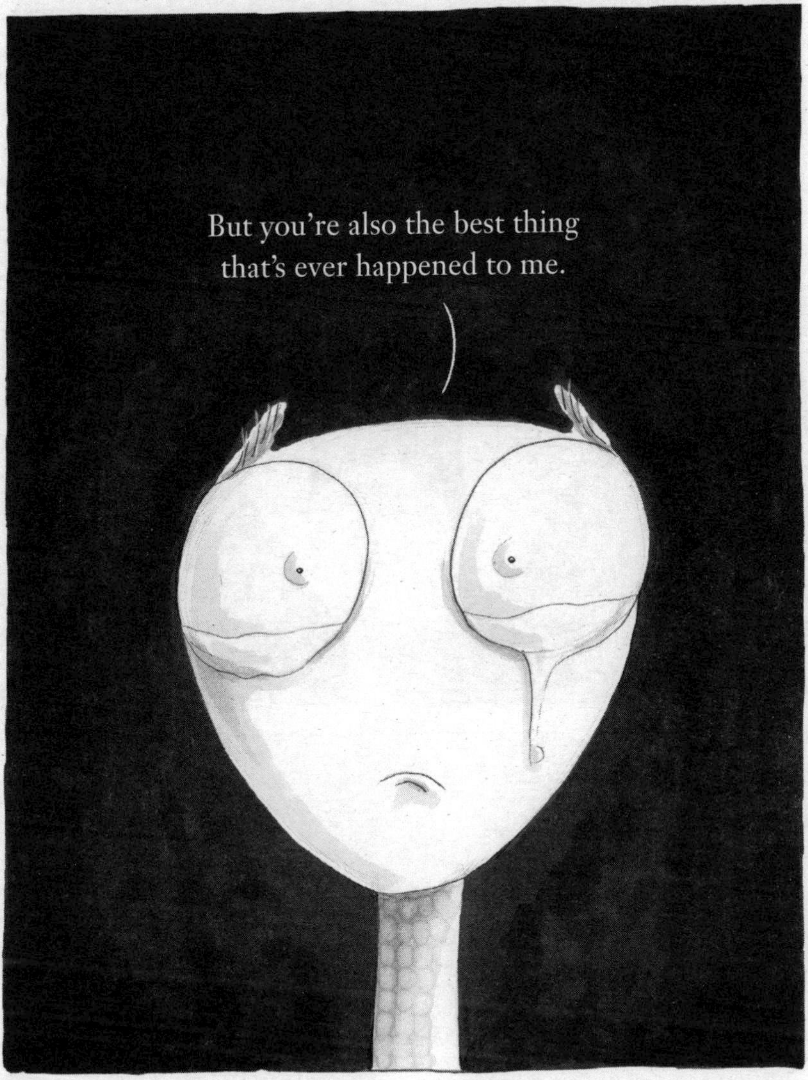
But you're also the best thing
that's ever happened to me.

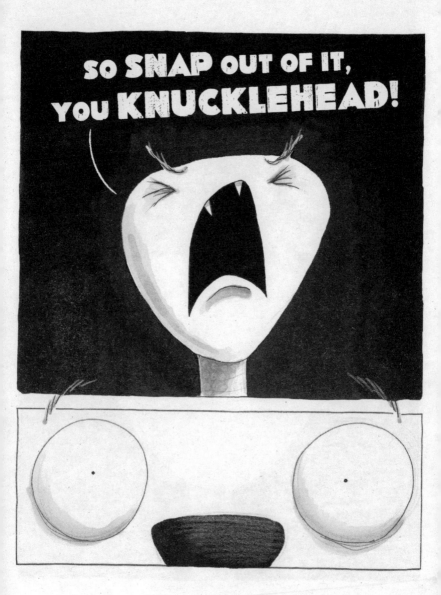

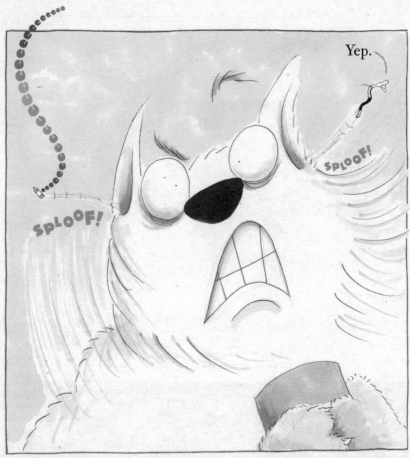

• CHAPTER 9 •
THE DARKEST HOUR

That's it, Butthands!
Let's blast up there and
take him down!

Whaaa . . . wait a minute!
My **SUPER SPEED** . . .
it's . . .

Gone. So is my power.

I CAN'T CHANGE.

He must have taken it all
away with that weird blast.

And why's he wearing a **CROWN**
all of a sudden?

GREAT QUESTION!
YOU MUST BE **BUSTING**
TO ASK ME **SO MANY THINGS**.

OH YES, I AGREE. YOU **ARE** BETTER LIKE THAT, MR VELOCIRAPTOR. JUST A BIG **DUMB** ANIMAL. LIKE ALL OF YOU.

SO, JUST TO RECAP—

YOUR **DINOSAUR** IS **STUPID** AGAIN, YOU'VE LOST ALL YOUR **SUPERPOWERS** AND... HMMM... WHAT WAS THAT OTHER THING?

...OH YES, OF COURSE...

YOUR LITTLE BUDDY **MR SNAKE** IS GONE **FOREVER!**

AHHHH.
THIS IS THE BEST DAY
EVAAAAAAHHHHH!!

TO BE CONCLUDED . . .

NOOOOOOO!

The bad guy can't win!

THE BAD GUYS have to win!

This is the one you've been waiting for—

the final instalment is on its way.

the BAD GUYS EPISODE 10

COMING SOON . . .

Psst!
Hey, guys? We're here . . .
we made it onto the Mothership.
Guys?!
Ah . . . guys?

AARON BLABEY

THE BAD GUYS

EPISODE 10
THE BADDEST DAY EVER

You know . . . I thought you didn't like him.

Are you serious?
He was the snake of my dreams.

Hang in there,
Agent Doom.

I am *so* misunderstood.

Howdy doody!

TIFFANY FLUFFIT, 6 News.

I'm a HUGE fan and I was wondering if you'd be prepared to give me an **EXCLUSIVE INTERVIEW** about the **'TRAGIC DEMISE OF MR SNAKE'**?

Whaddya say?

We're a bit busy at the moment.

• CHAPTER 1 •

MARMALADE THE CONQUEROR

YOU ARE MINE. FOR NOW AND FOREVER.

YOU'RE WELCOME. SERIOUSLY, DON'T MENTION IT.

SADLY, THE NAME OF MY PLANET CANNOT BE PRONOUNCED BY EARTHLINGS, BUT NEVERTHELESS YOU SHALL LOOK UPON IT WITH WONDER AND AWE . . .

YES!

I AM KDJFLOERHGCOINWERUHCGLEIRWFHEKLWJFHXALHW
CROWN PRINCE OF THE PLANET :(
AND BEFORE ME YOU SHALL KNEEL FOR ALL
ETERNITY!

That's very nice of you to say, but it is.

And because of it, Mr Snake is gone.

I hate that stupid name.

DON'T YOU DARE!

I have dedicated **MY LIFE** to the
INTERNATIONAL LEAGUE OF HEROES.
With these ladies right here,
I have fought so many battles and kept
the world safe for so long that I can
barely remember anything else.

Right, girls?

Uh huh.

I would *die* for the League of Heroes. Without hesitation. But know this—

I would be *proud* to be a member of the **GOOD GUYS CLUB.**

You would?!

The name doesn't matter. It's what you *do* that matters. And what you've all done is amazing. **I'D JOIN YOUR GANG ANY DAY.**

Me too, sugar.

Look, I can see where this is going, but I do have a real issue with the name. It's tragic.

Hear! Hear!

Then why don't we start a new organisation?

All of us. Together.

With a *cooler* name.

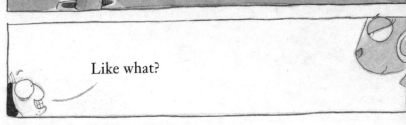

Like what?

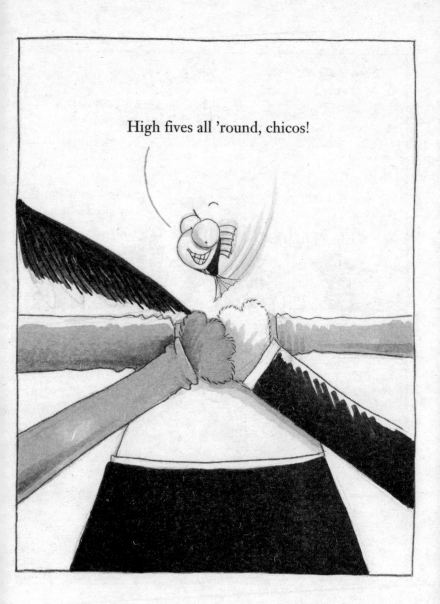

AWWW, ISN'T THAT CUTE!

IT'S REALLY CONVENIENT TOO— **STAY RIGHT THERE!** IT'LL MAKE IT SO MUCH EASIER TO **ANNIHILATE** YOU!

YOU WILL NEVER DEFEAT US!

REEEEEEALLY?
YOU HAVE NO SUPERPOWERS.
YOUR SPIRIT IS BROKEN.
AND, MOST IMPORTANTLY,
I'M UP HERE AND YOU'RE
DOWN THERE.
WHO COULD POSSIBLY
SAVE YOU?

CHAPTER 2

LEGS, THAT'S WHO

I need to get control of this ship.

And that's just what I'll do.

Rhonda?

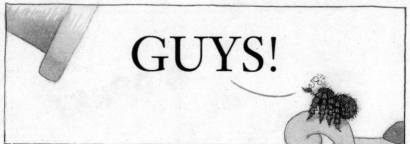

I hope you can hear me!
Rhonda can buy me some time but we're

MASSIVELY OUTNUMBERED.

We need your help.
Please, guys! Get up here!

WE NEED YOU!

Rhonda?
Who's *Rhonda?*

I'll tell you later. We have to

GET OUT OF HERE.

This is our chance!

· CHAPTER 3 ·
FROM BOLIVIA, WITH LOVE

You guys help as many civilians as you can. I'm going up there to help **LEGS AND RHONDA.**

Want some company?

Get up here, Mr Wolf.

Hey, chico?

Yeah?

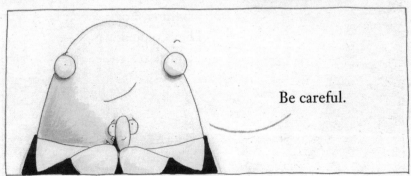

Be careful.

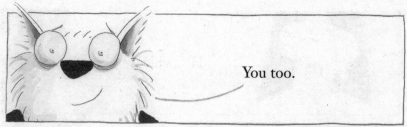

You too.

Watch the landing, Foxy. They come down a little rough!

So, now what?

Well sure—we're **OUTNUMBERED.** And no—you guys don't really have an **A-GAME** you can bring to this party. But you know what? **WE'VE GOT EACH OTHER'S BACKS.** And that's enough for me.

Plus, we've got ourselves a **REAL LIVE DINOSAUR.** That's something!

And I'm still really good at disguises. I'll just have to do it **'OLD SCHOOL'** without the superpowers.

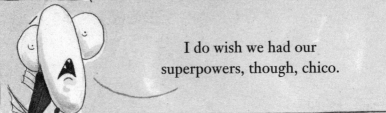

I do wish we had our superpowers, though, chico.

Pepe, who needs superpowers when you have **FAMILY?**

Papa?!

What are you doing
here, Papa?!

Your big brothers and cousins and I
thought you might like some help,

LITTLE PEPE.

Aaaah, they call me **MR PIRANHA** around here, Papa . . .

HAHAHAHAHA!

That's very good, Little Pepe. You've still got it.

CHAPTER 4

GETTING TO KNOW YOU

So this is what a mothership looks like on the inside. Surprisingly retro . . .

Whisper. They'll be everywhere . . .

That'll be Rhonda.
I'd better give her a hand . . .

Who *is* Rhonda?

It's Ellen.

Oh. Heh.
Er . . . hi . . .
Ellen.

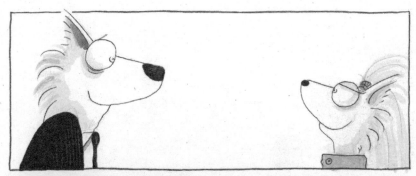

I'm Moe.

Well, Moe . . .

PECK!

I'll help Rhonda. You help Legs.

Meet you back here.

Are you OK?!

Yep.
It's only
a heart
attack . . .

I'm SO EXCITED you're here,
WOLFIE! Look! It's the
**CONTROLS TO
THE SHIP!**

So, the only
question is . . .

Where do you want
me to take her,
CAPTAIN?

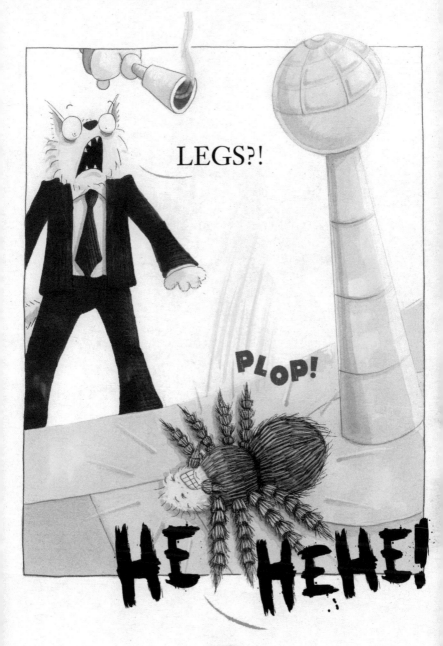

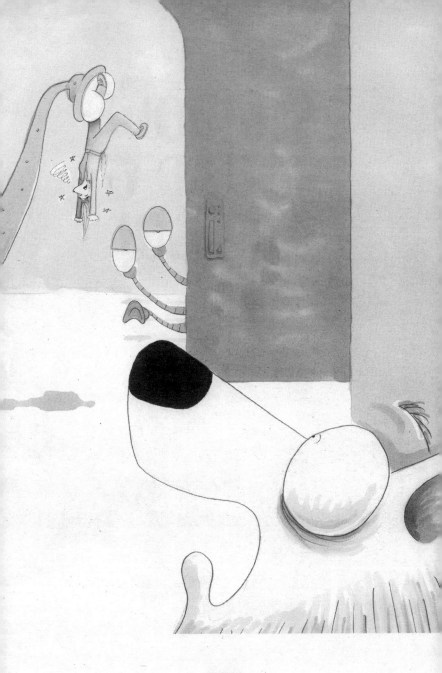

• CHAPTER 5 •

SHADOW SQUAD G ARE GO!

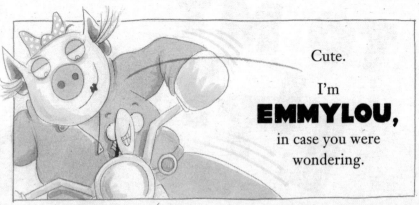

Cute.

I'm **EMMYLOU**, in case you were wondering.

And look at your **DADDY!**

Aliens!
Say hello . . .

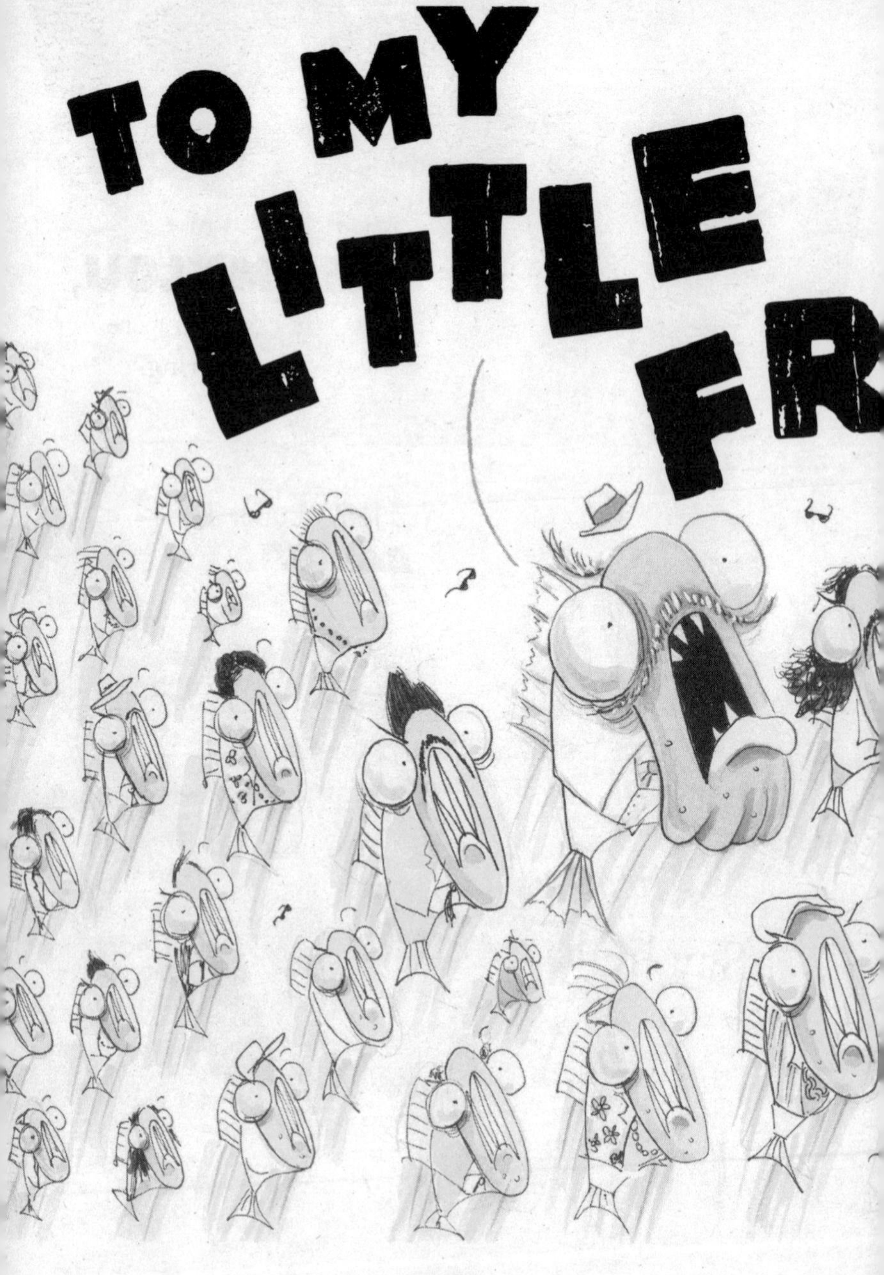
TO MY
LITTLE
FR

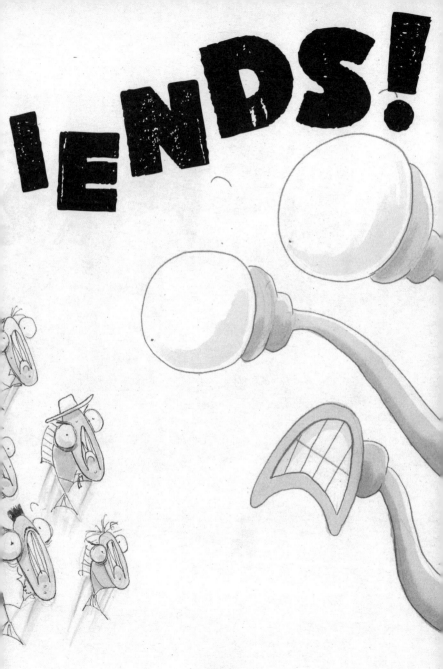

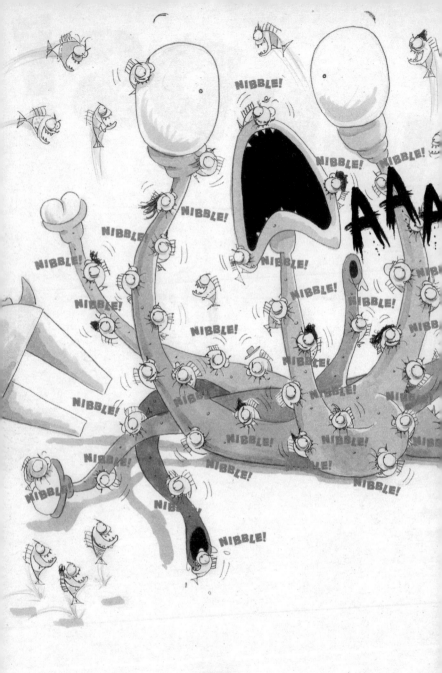

But man, I was *wrong*.

You know it, lady.

I think we might
just have a chance,
Pam, baby!

You go, girlfriend.

• CHAPTER 6 •

THE ROYAL LUNCHEON

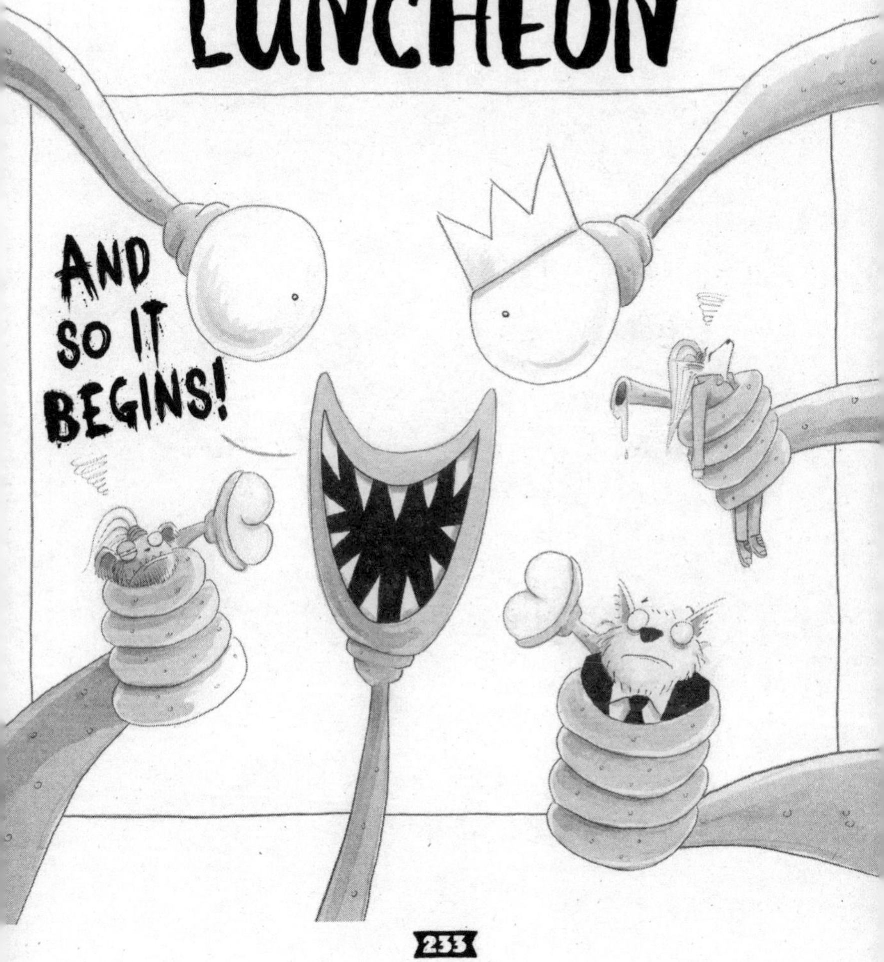

THE AGE OF ME!

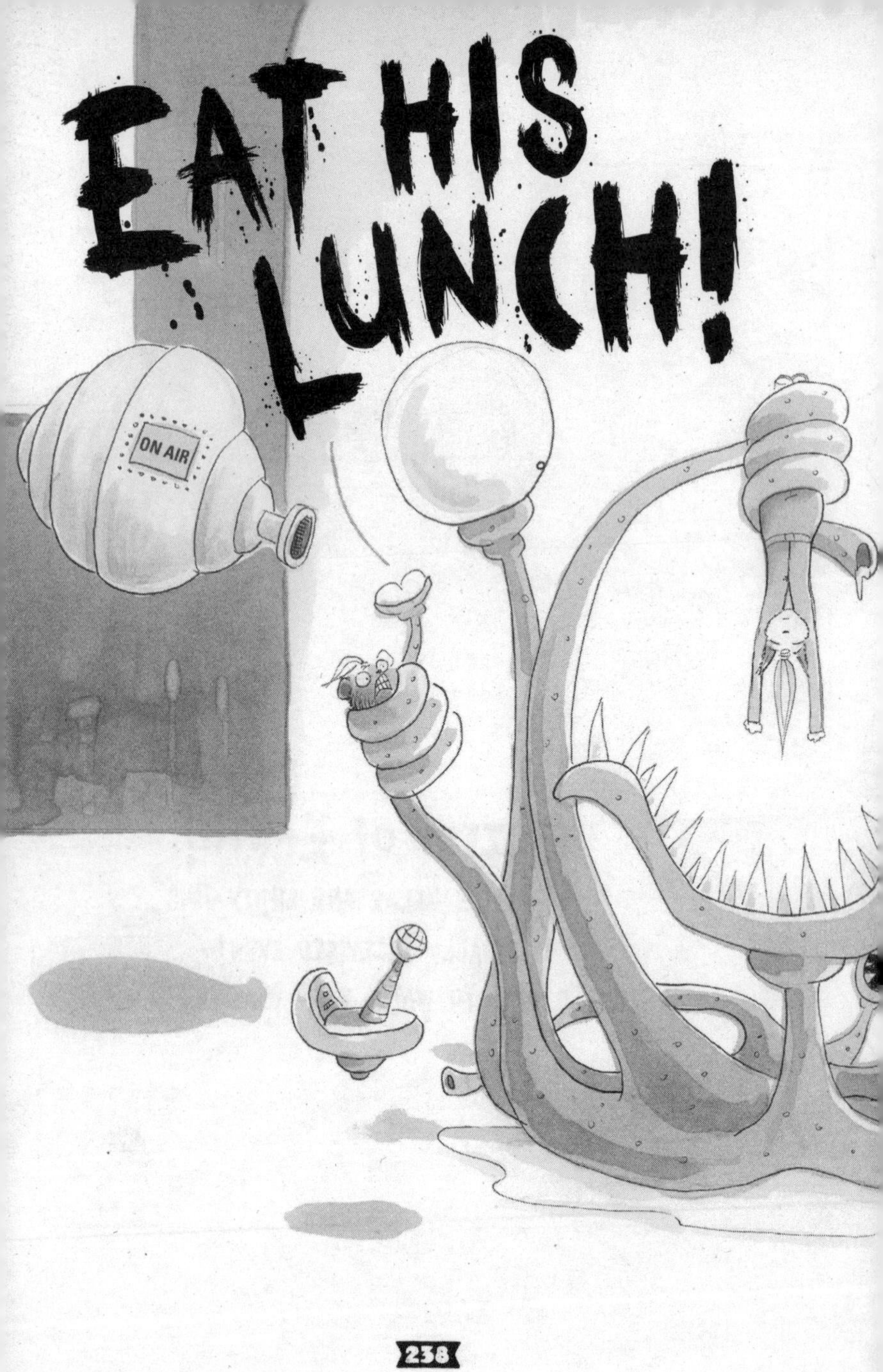
EAT HIS LUNCH!
ON AIR

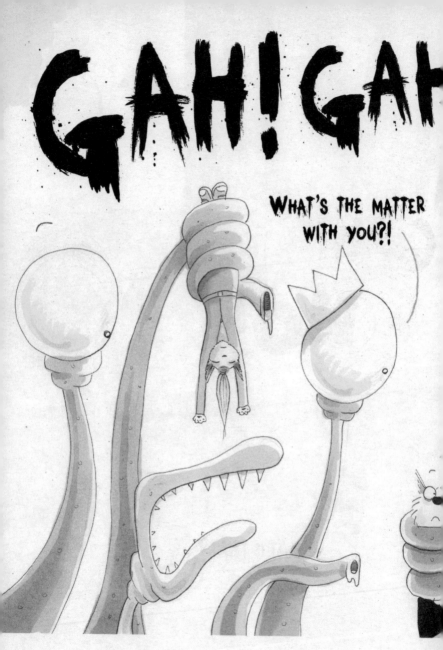

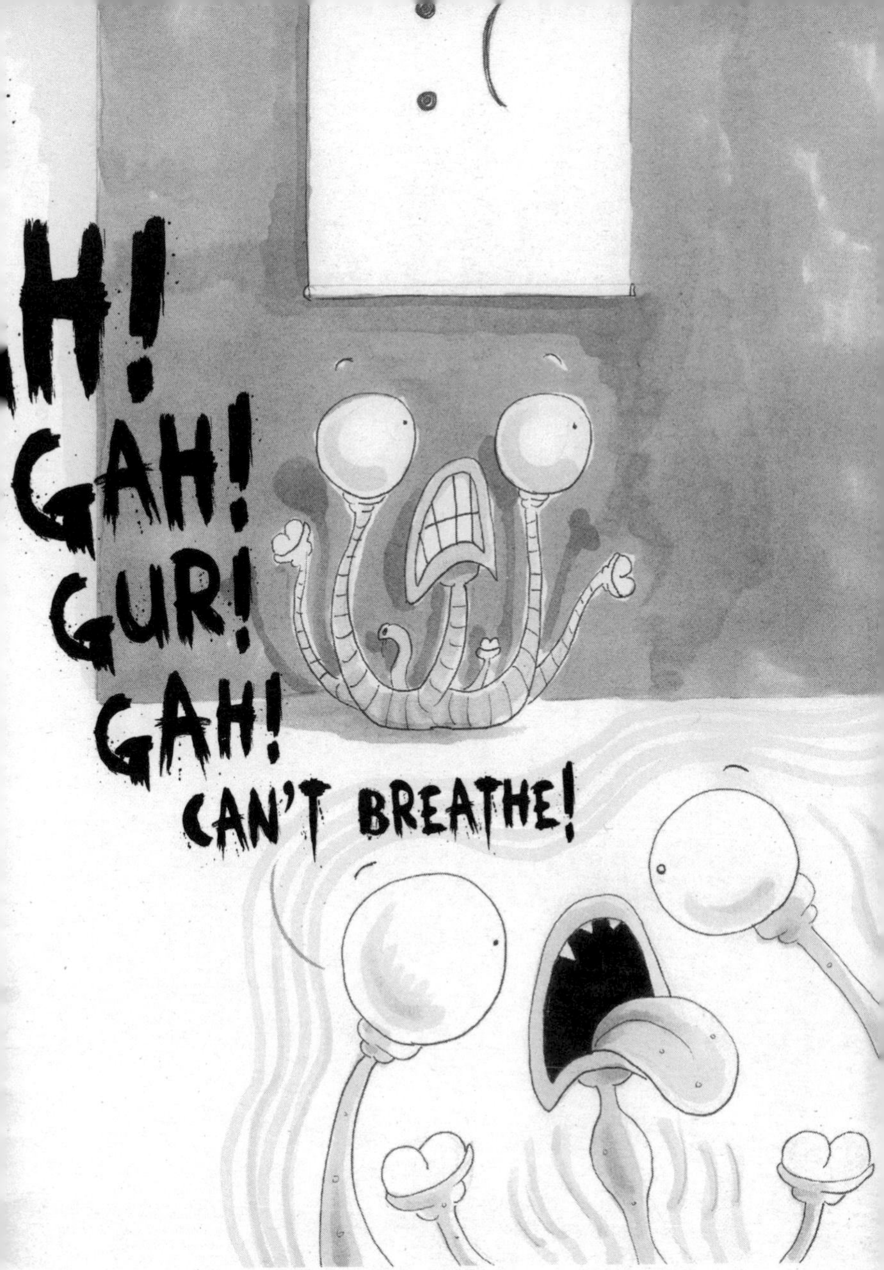
H!
GAH!
GUR!
GAH!
CAN'T BREATHE!

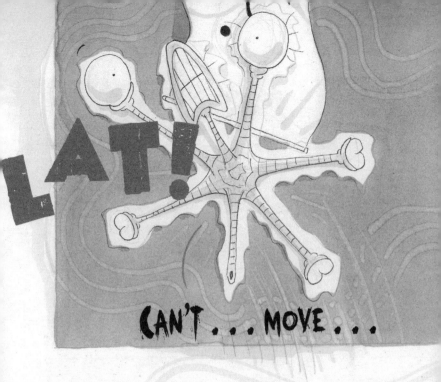

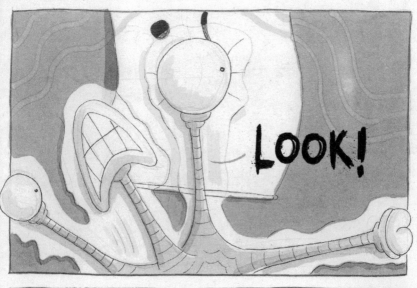

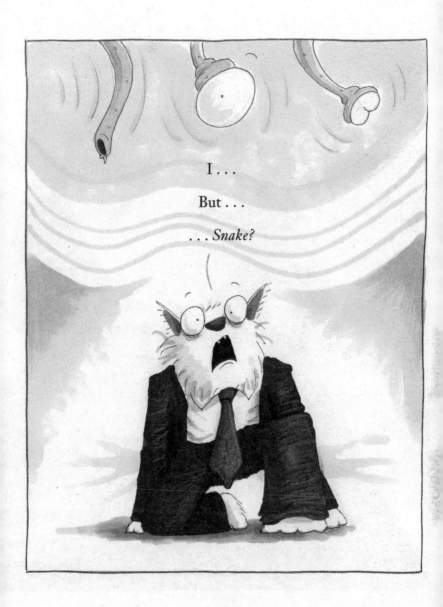

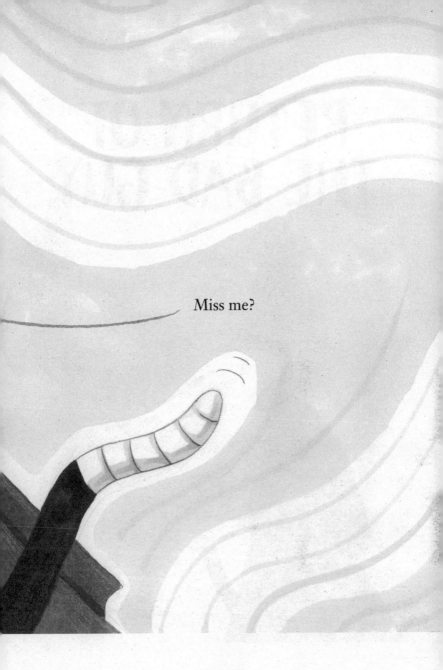

Miss me?

• CHAPTER 7 •
RETURN OF THE BAD GUY

GUARDS! STOP HIM, NOW!

Now, let's release
my friends.

FLICK!

CLUNK!

That's better.

THUD! THUD! THUD! THUD!

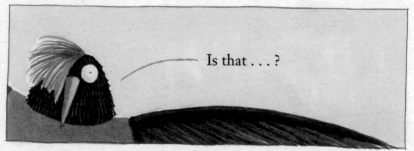

Is that . . . ?

So . . .

I saw you fall . . .

But did you see *where* I fell?

I fell into the
mothership's cannon . . .

just as the aliens started to
drain your superpowers.

And as they sucked in all
your powers . . .

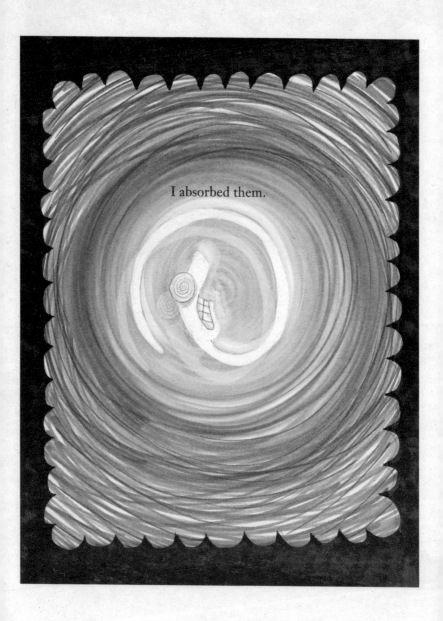

All of them.

And that probably makes **YOU** nervous, doesn't it?

You're probably thinking that I'll turn my **AWESOME POWER** against your **ENTIRE SPECIES** and get **SWEET REVENGE** for what you've done to Earth.

Right?

Well, I could do that . . .

But then it hit me . . .

I'm speaking now to
all the
ALIEN INVADERS!

My friends and I have made a terrible mistake.

Where's he going with *this*?!

We've been treating **YOU** the way others have been treating *us* our whole lives.

We decided that because **ONE** of you is a villain, you **ALL** must be.

We *assumed* you were **ALL** **DIRTY, ROTTEN** **BAD GUYS.**

And then I heard it . . .

Prince Marmalade.

PRINCE.

And that got
me thinking . . .

Well, thank you.
Thank you *very much*.

Now . . .

here's the big question . . .

CHAPTER 8

THE SAD TALE OF KDJFLOER ETC....

Hermano!
You're here! You're
here! You're here!

We can't believe
you're here!

Yeah, he's here. Geez.
Get *over* it.

I like your T-shirt.

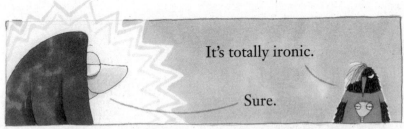

And Rhonda.

Stevie and Rhonda!
We make such a great team!

PAT!
PAT!
PAT!

I'M **NATHAN.** MARMALADE'S HEAD OF SECURITY.

You don't have to use a fake Earth name anymore. What's your real **ALIEN NAME?**

IT'S NATHAN.

I JUST WANTED TO APOLOGISE AND TRY TO EXPLAIN A LITTLE BIT ABOUT WHAT'S BEEN GOING DOWN...

YOU SEE, ON **OUR PLANET**, WE ALL LIVE FOR **THOUSANDS** OF YEARS. AND EVEN THOUGH **PRINCE MARMALADE IS 900** YEARS OLD, TO US HE'S STILL **A KID**. I MEAN, HE HAS THE EMOTIONAL MATURITY OF A **PRE-SCHOOLER**.

I'M **NOT** KIDDING. HE **LITERALLY** GOES TO PRE-SCHOOL.

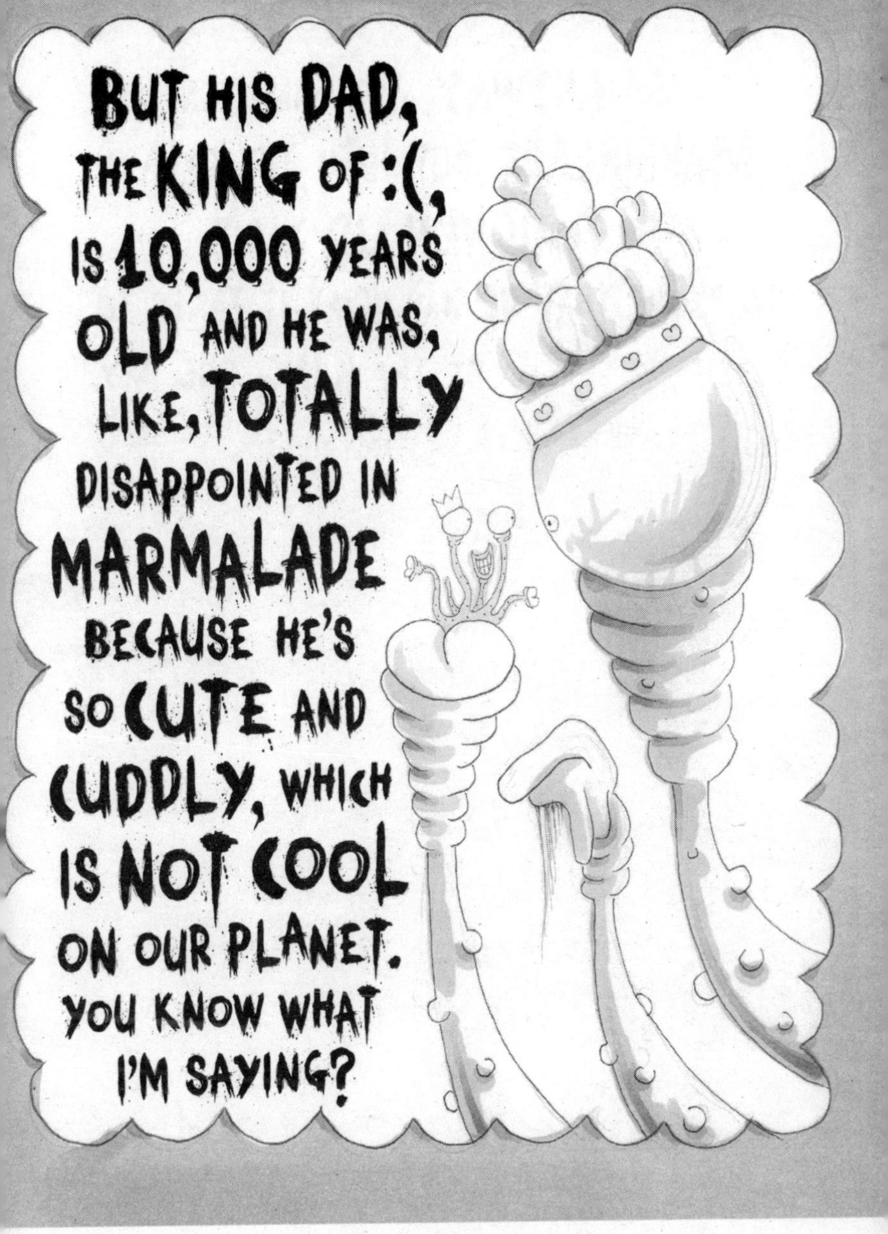
BUT HIS DAD, THE KING OF :(, IS 10,000 YEARS OLD AND HE WAS, LIKE, TOTALLY DISAPPOINTED IN MARMALADE BECAUSE HE'S SO CUTE AND CUDDLY, WHICH IS NOT COOL ON OUR PLANET. YOU KNOW WHAT I'M SAYING?

SO ANYWAY, THE KING SENT MARMALADE OUT INTO THE GALAXY TO TOUGHEN UP A BIT— TO PROVE THAT HE HAS WHAT IT TAKES TO BE THE KING ONE DAY.

AND HE SENT US WITH HIM, TO MAKE SURE HE WAS OK. BUT MARMALADE IS **SUCH A LITTLE BULLY.** HE WAS LIKE '**CONQUER THIS!**' AND '**ANNIHILATE THAT!**'

I MEAN WE ARE JUST, LIKE, TOTALLY **OVER** HIM.

SO, YOU KNOW . . . THANKS. AND WE PROMISE TO TAKE HIM TO SOME OTHER GALAXY. **FAR, FAR AWAY.** SO . . . HOPEFULLY . . . **NO HARD FEELINGS?**

COOLIO . . .

Hey, there is one thing . . .

ANYTHING!

· CHAPTER 9 ·
A VERY GOOD DAY

Here's the moment you've all been waiting for, and . . . **YES!** Here they are - with a *brand-new name!* I give you . . .

Wow, what a name!

You can practically see the logo!

YOU GUYS ROCK!

Oh, aren't I the giddy goat . . .

Apologies everyone!

These suits were NOT designed with 6-inch retractable claws in mind. I'm afraid I've shredded a couple putting them on . . .

It's good to have you back, Mr Snake.

It's good to be back,
Mr Wolf.

Time to take a bow . . .

LOVE YOU!

THE

...OR

IS IT?

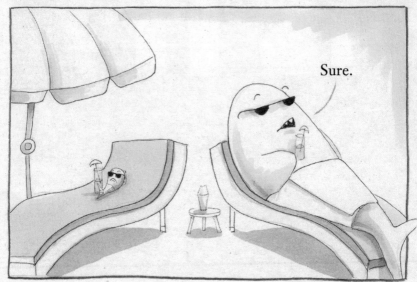

Does it worry you that
Mr Snake is suddenly
so powerful . . .

Nope.

What could possibly go
wrong with *that?*

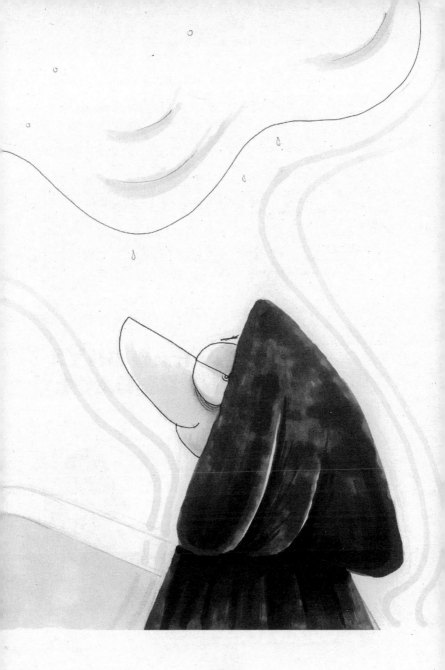

**THE BAD GUYS
WILL BE BACK.**